Dinosaur Christmas

by
Jerry Pallotta

CARTWHEEL BOOKS
An Imprint of Scholastic Inc.

Illustrated by
Howard McWilliam

A merry Christmas to Dr. Annekathryn Goodman.
— J.P.

For Rebecca, with love.
— H.W.

Text copyright © 2011 by Jerry Pallotta.
Illustrations copyright © 2011 by Howard McWilliam.

All rights reserved. Published by Scholastic Inc.
SCHOLASTIC, CARTWHEEL BOOKS, and associated logos are trademarks and/or registered trademarks of Scholastic Inc.

Library of Congress Cataloging-in-Publication Data

Pallotta, Jerry.
Dinosaur Christmas / by Jerry Pallotta ; illustrated by Howard McWilliam.
p. cm.
Originally published: New York : Scholastic, c2011.
Summary: After he gets a postcard from a little girl, Santa Claus reminisces about all the trouble he had when dinosaurs pulled his sleigh.
ISBN 978-0-545-43360-0
1. Santa Claus--Juvenile fiction. 2. Dinosaurs--Juvenile fiction. 3. Christmas stories.
[1. Santa Claus--Fiction. 2. Dinosaurs--Fiction. 3. Christmas--Fiction.]
I. McWilliam, Howard, 1977- ill. II. Title.

PZ7.P1785Din 2013
[E]--dc23

2012040593

10 9 8 7 6   20

Printed in Malaysia 108
This edition first printing, September 2013

Reindeer are great at their jobs.

But I remember the good old days . . .

. . . when dinosaurs pulled my sleigh.

Triceratops were
steady and ready . . .
but a bit slow.

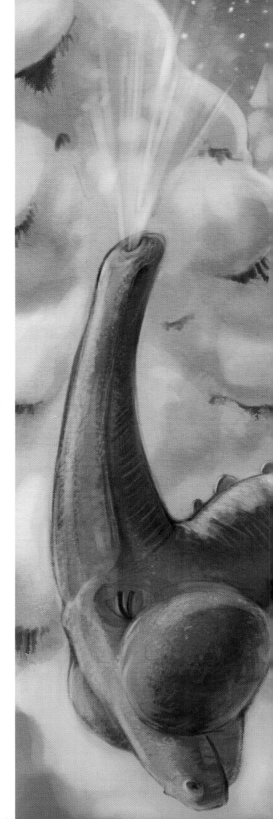

So I tried Parasaurolophus.

They tooted,
honked, and squeaked
too loud.

I tried Pterosaurs.
They flew so high.
Help! I couldn't breathe.

And those Velociraptors.

They were fidgety. *Stop slashing at each other!*

It was a gigantic-o
mistake-o!

And those Tyrannosaurus rex . . .

The Maiasauras were pretty and well behaved.

Until they ate the presents.
Bad dinosaurs!
I'm telling your mother!

Oh! And those Styracosaurus.

Pushy and way too bossy.

Then I tried
Stegosaurus.

It was a merry, spiky, pointy Christmas.

I tried Gallimimus.

They wouldn't stop dancing.

The Apatosaurus
worked well.

They were great
for deliveries and
seeing ahead.

Ankylosaurus,
Zephyrosaurus,
Nodosaurus —
  they never bored us.

Today the dinosaurs are gone.

Now the reindeer are my helpers.
And they're a treasure.

But sometimes
I miss the
good old days.

Merry
Christmas!

DEC   2020